Flynn, the red fire engine, was at the Sodor Rescue Centre. Diesel pulled up beside him.

"Good morning!" said Flynn.

"It isn't a good morning," moaned Diesel. "I'm very **busy!** You're not busy."

"I am waiting to get busy," said Flynn. He always wanted to be **Really Useful.**

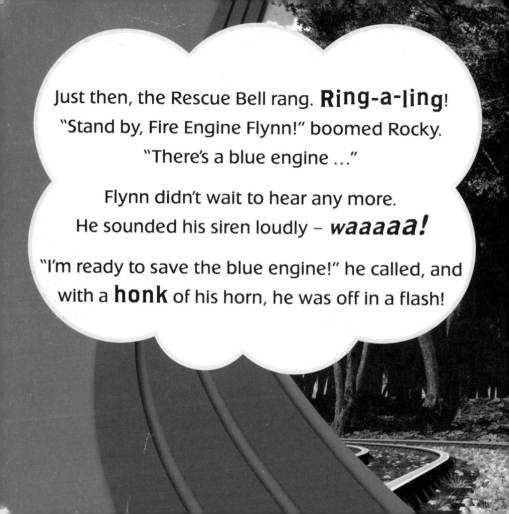

Just then, the Rescue Bell rang. **Ring-a-ling**!
"Stand by, Fire Engine Flynn!" boomed Rocky.
"There's a blue engine …"

Flynn didn't wait to hear any more.
He sounded his siren loudly – *waaaaa!*

"I'm ready to save the blue engine!" he called, and
with a **honk** of his horn, he was off in a flash!

"There's a blue engine in trouble!"
puffed Flynn as he raced down the track.
When he saw Edward, the blue engine,
he **screeched** to a stop.

"Edward, I've come to save you!"
he called. "Fire Engine Flynn to the rescue!"

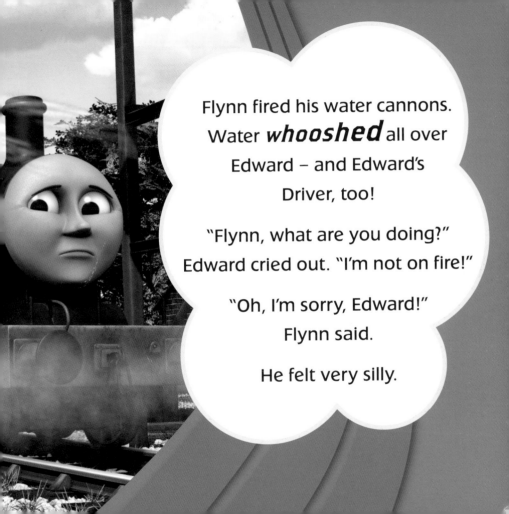

Flynn fired his water cannons. Water ***whooshed*** all over Edward – and Edward's Driver, too!

"Flynn, what are you doing?" Edward cried out. "I'm not on fire!"

"Oh, I'm sorry, Edward!" Flynn said.

He felt very silly.

"It must be another blue engine that's in trouble," said Flynn. "I must hurry to find it!"

And Flynn **rushed** away.

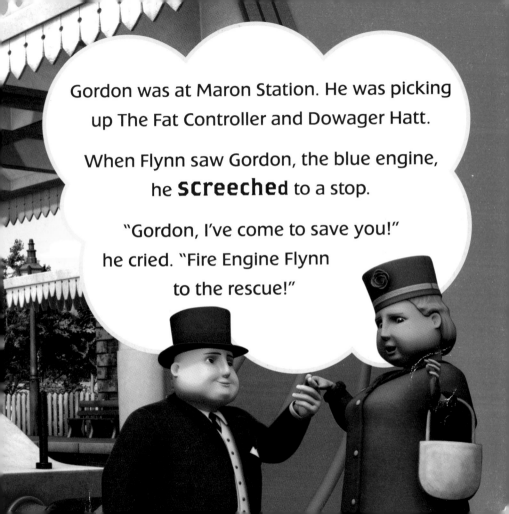

Gordon was at Maron Station. He was picking up The Fat Controller and Dowager Hatt.

When Flynn saw Gordon, the blue engine, he **screeched** to a stop.

"Gordon, I've come to save you!" he cried. "Fire Engine Flynn to the rescue!"

Flynn fired his water cannons.
Water **splashed** all over
Gordon and The Fat Controller!

"I'm not on fire, Flynn!"
Gordon grumbled.

Flynn had tried to save the
wrong engine again!
He felt very
silly indeed.

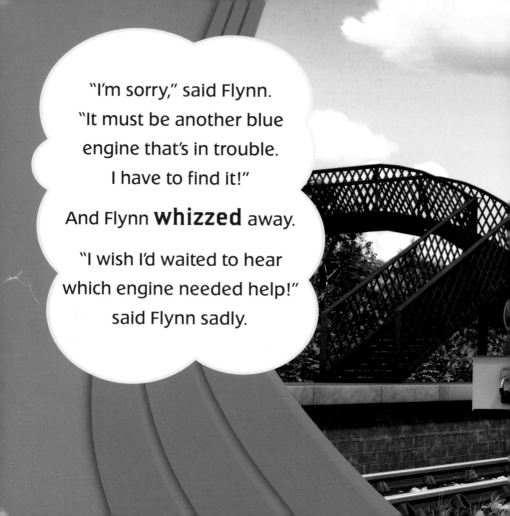

"I'm sorry," said Flynn.
"It must be another blue
engine that's in trouble.
I have to find it!"

And Flynn **whizzed** away.

"I wish I'd waited to hear
which engine needed help!"
said Flynn sadly.

Flynn found another blue engine at the Dieselworks. It was Thomas. His firebox was on **fire!**

Flynn fired his water cannons.

But no water came out! Flynn had used it all up.

"Sorry, Thomas," Flynn said, sadly. "I didn't wait to hear which blue engine I had to save, and **now** I can't save you!"

Then Flynn had a great idea. "Diesels," he said, "**you** will save Thomas!"

So the Diesels' Drivers poured water on Thomas' flaming firebox. And with a **fizz**, the fire went out.

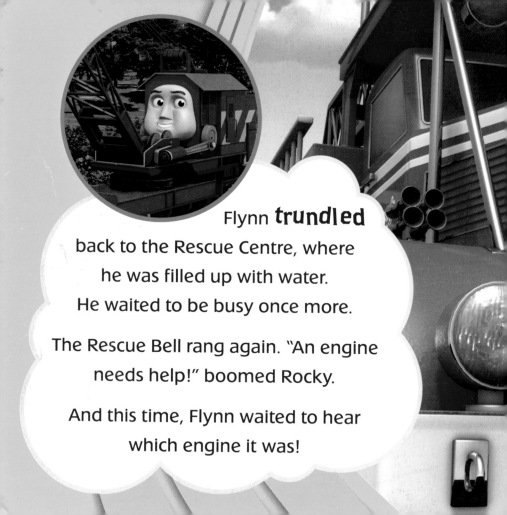

Flynn **trundled** back to the Rescue Centre, where he was filled up with water. He waited to be busy once more.

The Rescue Bell rang again. "An engine needs help!" boomed Rocky.

And this time, Flynn waited to hear which engine it was!

PEEP! PEEP!

The End

THOMAS & FRIENDS™

Fire Engine Flynn